Storyteller Tales

The Noisy Stable
and other Christmas stories

Over the centuries, the Christmas stories
in the Bible have been passed on from
generation to generation. These delightful
retellings capture the joy, wonder and
celebration that surrounded the birth of
a very special baby, Jesus.

Bob Hartman is a widely acclaimed
author and storyteller. He is best known
for *The Lion Storyteller Bible* and other books
in the *Storyteller* series in which these tales
were originally published.

Other titles in this series

The Noisy Stable

and other Christmas stories

Bob Hartman

Illustrations by
Brett Hudson

LION
CHILDREN'S

Published by Lion Children's Books
an imprint of
Lion Hudson plc
Wilkinson House, Jordan Hill Road,
Oxford OX2 8DR, England
www.lionhudson.com/lionchildrens
ISBN 978 0 7459 4824 9

First edition 2004

Acknowledgments
These stories were first published in
The Lion Storyteller Bedtime Book and
The Lion Storyteller Book of Animal Tales

A catalogue record for this book is available
from the British Library

Contents

*All these retellings are based on stories in the first four books
of the New Testament part of the Bible.*

A Surprise for Zechariah

Gabriel was an angel. A very busy angel.

God decided that the time had come to send his Son into the world. So he chose Gabriel to get everything ready.

The first thing Gabriel did was to visit an old priest called Zechariah. He and his wife, Elizabeth, had no children of their own. And that made them very sad. So, one day, while Zechariah was working in the temple in

Jerusalem, Gabriel appeared to him – bright
and shiny, glowing and gold!

Zechariah had never seen an angel
before, so he was very frightened. His legs
turned to jelly. He quivered, he shivered and
he shook.

'Don't be afraid,' said Gabriel gently. 'For I am here to bring you good news! You and your wife have been praying for a child, and soon your prayers will be answered. You will have a baby. You will call him John. And when he grows up, he will help the world get ready to meet God's own special Son!'

'But my wife and I are so old. How can we possibly have a child?' said Zechariah.

'I'll prove it to you,' said Gabriel with a smile. 'From now until the time the child is born, you will not be able to speak a word. That way you will know what I say is true.'

Zechariah opened his mouth to answer the angel. But nothing came out. Not a word. Not a whisper. Not a sound!

So he staggered out of the temple – eyes wide open and lips shut tight. And it wasn't long before his wife came to him with the most amazing news.

'I'm going to have a baby!' she cried, tears of joy streaming down her face. 'After all these years, our prayers have been answered!'

Zechariah wanted to say, 'I know.' He wanted to say, 'The angel told me this would happen.' He wanted to shout 'Hooray!' But all he could do was smile. And that smile said more than enough!

A Surprise for Mary

That busy angel Gabriel went to work again.

Six months after Elizabeth discovered that she would have a child, he visited Elizabeth's cousin, Mary.

Mary and Elizabeth were quite different.

Elizabeth lived in the south, near the big city of Jerusalem. But Mary lived further north, in a little town called Nazareth.

Elizabeth was old. But Mary was young.

And Elizabeth had been married for many years, but Mary had never been married at all. She was engaged, however, to a carpenter named Joseph.

Mary was in her house, one day, dreaming of the wedding and the life that she and Joseph would share together. And that's when Gabriel appeared to her – bright and shiny, glowing and gold – just as he'd appeared to old Zechariah.

'Hello, Mary,' Gabriel said. 'God is with you and wants to do something very special for you.'

Mary didn't know what to think. She had never seen an angel before. And as for God wanting to do something special for her, well, she couldn't imagine what that might

be. She was too scared to ask, and Gabriel could see the worry in her eyes.

'There's no need to be afraid,' he told her. 'God has chosen you for something wonderful. He wants you to be the mother of a little baby, a baby called Jesus.'

Mary looked more worried than ever. And puzzled too.

'I don't understand,' she said. 'How can I have a baby when I don't yet have a husband?'

Gabriel smiled. It was a warm smile. And a mysterious smile too.

'God's own Spirit will visit you,' he said. 'Like a welcome shadow on a warm summer's day, he will cover you and wrap himself around you. And the child who will spring to life in you will be God's child too.'

Mary was shaking now. Her eyes were wide open, amazed. Her mouth dropped open too. She had never heard anything like this before!

'I know this is hard to believe,' Gabriel went on. 'But God can do the most amazing things. Why, your own cousin, Elizabeth – that's right, Elizabeth, who could never have a child before – is expecting a baby too! Impossible? Not for God! So what do you say, Mary? Will you be the mother of God's Son?'

Mary shut her eyes. She shut her mouth too. She looked just as if she was praying.

What will Joseph think, she wondered, when he hears about the child? He is bound to think the worst. And my parents too.

Their plans, all their plans, will be ruined! And yet, God has a plan as well. And he has chosen me – me of all people – to be a part of that plan. What can I do but say yes?

And so Mary nodded. Eyes still shut, head bowed in prayer, she nodded.

'I will do it,' she said. 'I will be the mother of God's Son.'

And when she opened her eyes, the angel was gone.

Mary had to tell someone!

The news that the angel Gabriel had given her was so amazing that it seemed almost too good to be true. So Mary hurried to visit the one person in the world she thought would understand – her cousin, Elizabeth.

Elizabeth was expecting a child of her

own, remember? It was the son that Gabriel (that busy angel!) had promised to her and her husband, Zechariah.

Mary said 'Hello' to her cousin. But instead of saying 'Hello' back, Elizabeth said a surprised 'Ooh!'

'It's my baby!' she chuckled. 'When you said, 'Hello' he jumped! He jumped for joy,

inside me! He knows – don't you see? – that the baby who is growing inside you is God's own Son.'

Elizabeth knew! She already knew! Even before Mary could tell her. Now Mary was more amazed than ever.

'God has done something wonderful for you,' said Elizabeth to Mary. 'And you have to trust that it will all come true – just as the angel told you.'

Mary nodded, 'I do. I really do.' And then she paused. And then she thought. And then she spoke again – as if she was making up a poem, or singing her own special song:

God has been so good to me
And I simply don't deserve it.
I'm nothing. A nobody.
Yet God has chosen me
To be the mother of his Son!

And one day – I'm sure of this –
Everyone will know my name
And be able to tell my story.
That's how God works, isn't it?
He knocks down the mighty and proud
And lifts up those who are small and weak.
He sends the rich away hungry.
And he feeds the hungry until they're full!
He has watched over his people, Israel,
From the time of our father, Abraham.
And now, praise God, he's watching over me!

When she had finished, Mary hugged her cousin, Elizabeth. Then she stayed with her for three months more, until Elizabeth's baby, John, was born, and then returned to her home in Nazareth.

A Name for the Baby

What will you call him? Tell us his name!'

That's what everyone wanted to know: Elizabeth's sisters and brothers. Her nieces and nephews. Her cousins and neighbours and friends.

They had all come round to celebrate the birth of her son. They knew how long she had prayed. They knew how long she had waited. They had shared her surprised delight when she discovered that she would be having a child at last. And now they wanted to know his name.

'Perhaps you will name him after dear Uncle Ezra,' suggested one of her sisters.

'Or Grandfather Saul,' suggested another. 'Look! He has his smile!'

'Or what about our father?' added one of her brothers. 'It would be such an honour!'

And that's when Elizabeth held up her hand. 'We have already decided on a name,' she announced. 'We will call him John.'

The room went quiet for a moment.

And then Elizabeth's oldest sister asked the question that everyone wanted to hear. 'But why do that? No one in our family has ever been called John.'

And that's when Elizabeth turned to her husband, Zechariah. He had been sitting there quietly (for that busy angel Gabriel had taken away his voice – remember?).

Zechariah nodded and smiled a mysterious smile. Then he picked up a writing tablet and wrote on it, clearly, so that everyone could see, 'His name is John.' And the minute he did so, Zechariah could speak again!

'Praise God!' he shouted. And he didn't stop talking until he had told them everything about the angel's visit and God's promise and how Gabriel had told him

exactly what the child's name would be.

'This boy will be something special!' he concluded. 'God has great plans for him.'

And so God did. For when little John grew

up, he went to live in the wilderness. He ate locusts for his supper and wild honey for his dessert. And he told God's people to change their ways and to be sorry for the wrong things that they had done, so that they would be ready to meet God's own special Son.

Joseph's Dream

Joseph the carpenter was not very happy. Not very happy at all. The girl he had planned to marry was going to have a baby, but the baby was not his.

Mary had tried to explain. She had told him about the angel and what the angel had said. She had told him that the baby would be God's special Son. But Joseph did not believe her. And who could blame him? For the story was so amazing that Mary hardly believed it herself!

In the end, Joseph decided to call off the wedding – quietly, of course, so that Mary would not be embarrassed. And that was when that busy angel, Gabriel, decided to make another visit.

He appeared to Joseph in a dream – bright and shiny, glowing and gold – deep in the middle of the night.

'There's no need to be worried,' he said to Joseph. 'There's no need to be afraid. Everything Mary has told you is true. The baby she is carrying is God's own special Son. When he is born, God wants you to call him Jesus. His name means "God saves". And when he grows up, that is exactly what he will do. He will be "God among us",

"God come to save us" from everything that is wicked and wrong.'

When Joseph woke up, he knew exactly what to do. He went straight to Mary's house. He hugged her and told her he was sorry that he had not believed her. Then, just as soon as he could, he married her. And he took her home to be his wife.

Time to Be Counted

Mary counted the months.

One, two, three.

Four, five, six.

Seven, eight and nine.

It was almost time for her baby to be born!

Mary counted the blankets. Mary counted the towels. And then Mary smiled. For everything was ready – ready for the birth of God's own special Son.

But somebody else was counting too. And all Mary's plans were about to be ruined.

'It's the Emperor!' sighed Joseph, as he walked into the house. 'He wants to count everyone in the country. Everyone! And to make it easy for him, we have to go back to my home town.'

'Your home town?' cried Mary. 'But that means we have to go all the way to…'

'… Bethlehem!' sighed Joseph again.

'A week's journey, at least! And you with the baby coming.'

'I can't do it,' wept Mary. And the tears rolled down her cheeks.

One, two, three.

Four, five, six.

Seven, eight and nine.

Joseph counted each tear. Then he wiped them all away.

'But you must,' he said gently. 'It's the law.'

Then he held her and kissed her and he added more gently still, 'God is with you. Remember? That's what the angel told you. And if God is with you, then he will help you to make this journey. It's his promise,' said Joseph with a smile. 'So you can count on it!'

A Long Journey

One, two, three.

Four, five, six.

Seven, eight and nine.

Mary counted the miles. And the donkey's footsteps. And the number of times the little baby kicked inside her belly.

It was a long trip. And a hot trip. And she prayed that it would soon be over.

One, two, three.

Four, five, six.

Seven, eight and nine.

Mary knew, because she counted, that there were many more miles to go.

When they arrived, at last, in Bethlehem, Mary and Joseph looked for a place to stay.

One, two, three.

Four, five, six.

Seven, eight and nine.

They knocked on door after door.

But at every door, the answer was the same. 'We have no room here! Go away!'

Mary began to cry.

'It's the baby!' she wept. 'The baby is coming. And I need somewhere to rest.'

So Joseph looked up and down the street once more.

One, two, three.

Four, five, six.

Seven, eight and nine.

And there, at house number ten, he found a door he had missed!

The door opened. The innkeeper smiled. But when Joseph asked if he had an empty room, the innkeeper sadly shook his head.

'Bethlehem is bursting,' he said with a sigh. 'We have no room at all.'

'But my wife…' Joseph pleaded. 'My wife is about to have a baby.'

'I can see that,' the innkeeper nodded. 'But I'm sorry, there's nothing I can do.' And he started to close the door.

'Please!' Joseph cried.

'Please!' wept Mary as well.

And that's when the door swung open again.

'There is a place,' nodded the innkeeper. 'Back behind the inn. It's nothing fancy,

mind you. But it's warm and clean and dry.
And you can have your baby safely there.'

So he led them to the stable. And there,
among the animals, Mary finally lay down
and gave birth to God's own special Son.

The Noisy Stable

It was nothing special. Just an ordinary
stable. Filled with ordinary stable sounds.

The deep 'moo' of a big black cow.

The noisy 'hee-haw' of a little brown
donkey.

The 'coo' of a dove, the 'baa' of a lamb,
and the 'scrickety-scrack' of a spider,
skittering along the wall.

But then there came another sound. An

out-of-the-ordinary sound. A sound that had never been heard in this stable before the sharp 'waa-waa!' of a newborn baby.

It was Mary's baby, of course. The baby the angel Gabriel had promised her. But there was nothing ordinary about him. For he was Jesus, God's own special Son.

The cow went 'moo'.

The donkey brayed 'hee-haw'.

The dove called 'coo', the lamb cried 'baa', and the spider skittered, 'scrickety-scrack', back into his web.

It was just an ordinary stable. With ordinary stable sounds…

And one extraordinary baby boy!

A Flock of Angels

That busy angel, Gabriel, had one more Christmas job to do. He had to tell somebody that the baby, Jesus, had been born.

He could have told a powerful somebody – like the king.

He could have told a religious somebody – like the high priest.

Or he could have told a wealthy somebody – like the richest man in Bethlehem.

But instead he told the shepherds – plain and ordinary somebodies. Somebodies like you and me!

They were watching their sheep, out on a hillside. It was late. It was dark. And some of them just wanted to drop off to sleep.

And that's when Gabriel appeared – bright and shiny, glowing and gold – just as he had appeared to Mary and to Zechariah.

'Don't be afraid!' he said to the shepherds, and he smiled when he realized how silly that sounded.

Of course they were afraid! Who wouldn't be? They had never seen an angel before.

And so they were trembling and shaking, just like frightened sheep.

'I have good news for you!' Gabriel explained. 'God has sent someone very special, to bring joy to this dark world. And tonight that someone has been born – not far from here in Bethlehem! Go, and you will find him, a baby bundled up tight and lying in a manger.'

And then, suddenly, Gabriel was not alone.

The angels that joined him looked like sheep, at first, bright against the dark sky- reflections of the beasts on the hill below. But as the shepherds watched, the angels spread their wings and began to sing:

'Glory to God in heaven,

And peace to men on earth!'

And when they had finished, they disappeared, leaving the shepherds alone.

It took no time at all. The shepherds leaped to their feet and went to Bethlehem. There they found Mary and Joseph, and the baby in the manger. And when they described what they had seen – to the innkeeper and his wife and anyone else who would listen – everyone wondered and was

amazed. Everyone but Mary, that is, who nodded and smiled as if she had expected just this sort of thing to happen.

Then, singing and laughing, the shepherds went back to the hills. But they kept their eyes trained on the sky, just in case another bright flock of angels should appear!

The Star That Went Zoom!

Twinkle – twinkle, went the stars. And the star-watchers nodded and smiled.

'There's a pretty one!' the first star-watcher said.

'And look how brightly that one is shining,' said the second star-watcher.

'And the big one – the big one over there,' cried the third star-watcher. 'I don't think I've ever seen one so huge!'

Twinkle-twinkle, went the stars. And then one of the stars went Zoom!

'Did you see that?' asked the first star-watcher.

'Couldn't miss it!' said the second.

'What do you suppose it means?' wondered the third.

So they all ran for their special star-watching books.

Twinkle-twinkle, went the stars. And the star-watchers read and searched and scratched their heads. 'It's not an earthquake,' said the first star-watcher. 'We can be grateful for that!'

'And it's not a flood, either,' said the second.

That's when the third star-watcher went 'Aha! I've found it! A zooming star means that, somewhere, a new king has been born!'

'But where?' asked the other star-watchers.

'There's no way to tell,' said the third star-watcher, 'unless we follow the star and see where it stops.'

'Then let's do it!' said the first star-watcher, putting on his hat.

'Sounds good to me,' said the second, as

he pulled on his long coat.

'I'll need to find someone to mind the cat,' said the third. 'But I'd like to go as well.'

And so the star-watchers gathered their servants and loaded their camels. And with the stars twinkle-twinkling above, they set off after that special star – the star that went Zoom!

The star zoomed left. The star zoomed right. Over hills it zoomed, and deserts and rivers and mountain peaks.

The star-watchers did their best to zoom after it. But the hills were high, and the deserts were hot. The rivers were deep, and the mountain peaks were hard to climb. And that was why it took them so long to follow the star.

For days and weeks and months they

travelled, until finally the star stopped, and they found themselves in Judea, at the edge of the Great Sea.

'This is the land of the Jews,' said the first star-watcher.

'Then the baby must be their new king,' said the second.

'So let's find the palace,' suggested the third star-watcher, 'and give him the honour he deserves.'

They thought they had it all worked out, and so the star-watchers headed for

Jerusalem and the palace of the king. But what they failed to notice was that the star had zoomed somewhere else!

The star-watchers asked everyone they met.

'We have come from the East,' they explained. 'We are looking for a king. Perhaps you could help us find him – the newborn King of the Jews.'

Everyone was surprised by the question.

And no one more than King Herod. 'What do they mean?' he shouted at his advisers. 'I am the King of the Jews!'

'Y-Yes, of c-course,' stammered the frightened men. 'B-But perhaps they are looking for the special king – the one God promised us, many years ago.'

'And where would they find such a king?' Herod growled.

'In B-Bethlehem,' the advisers stammered again. 'At least, that's what the prophets say.'

'I see,' Herod muttered. And then his eyes began to twinkle-twinkle like two dark stars. 'Send for these star-watchers,' he commanded. 'I have something to ask them.'

The star-watchers came as quickly as they could. And once Herod had sent away his advisers, he leaned over to the star-watchers and whispered, 'The king you are looking for is in the town of Bethlehem. I want you to go there – it's not far – and when you

have found him, I want you to return and tell me exactly where he is – so that I might honour him too.'

The star – watchers nodded and bowed. They thanked the king and then headed straight for Bethlehem. But what they did not know was that Herod was an evil king – a king determined to kill anyone who tried to take his throne – even a little baby boy in Bethlehem!

Gifts for a King

When the star-watchers arrived in
Bethlehem, the star was already waiting for
them there. But it was no longer zooming.
Instead, it crept along slowly, leading them
through the narrow streets of the town. And
then, suddenly, it stopped, and hovered
silently over a very ordinary-looking house.

'This must be the place,' said the first star-
watcher.

'It doesn't look much like a palace,' said the second.

'Well, we shall have to go in and see for ourselves,' said the third. And he knocked, politely, on the door.

An ordinary-looking man opened the door – a man as ordinary as the house.

'We're very sorry,' said the first star-watcher. 'We must have the wrong place.'

'Forgive us for troubling you,' apologized the second.

'But the star…' whispered the third star-watcher to the others, 'The star is right overhead.' And then he turned to the man at the door. 'We're looking for a king – the newborn King of the Jews. I don't suppose you have a baby here?'

And with that, the ordinary-looking man smiled. A secret smile. A knowing smile.

For this man was Joseph.

'As a matter of fact, we do,' he said. 'Little Jesus is almost a year old, now, but I think he's the one you're looking for.'

The star-watchers filed into the house. The child was sitting on his mother's lap, playing with her fingers. And as soon as they saw him, they knew they were in the right place.

One by one, the star-watchers fell to
their knees before him. Then they gave him
presents – presents they had brought all the
way from the East. But they weren't the kind
of presents that most people give to babies.
No rattles or building blocks or soft toys.

No, they were presents fit for a king:

Bright, shiny gold.

A rich perfume called myrrh.

And frankincense, a sweet-smelling oil.

The baby patted the gold, and the jar that held the oil. But when he very nearly tipped over the bottle of perfume, his mother gently took his hand. 'Thank you,' she said to the star-watchers. 'It was kind of you to come.'

And so the star-watchers stood and bowed and said their goodbyes. It was too late to return to Jerusalem, so they set up their tents on the outskirts of town. But as they lay there asleep, each of the star-watchers had a dream. There was a visitor, bright and shiny, glowing and gold (that busy angel, Gabriel, perhaps?). And the visitor had a message.

'King Herod wants to kill the child,' the message warned them. 'You must not return to him. Go back to your homes, instead. Go quickly! And you will save the child's life.'

So the star-watchers rose at once. They folded their tents. They loaded their camels. And, rubbing the sleep from their eyes, they started for home, the stars twinkle-twinkling like gold to light their way.

King Herod's Evil Plan

King Herod frowned.

King Herod scowled.

King Herod clenched his teeth and scrunched up his face.

And then King Herod shouted. 'THE STAR-WATCHERS ARE GONE?!'

'Y-Yes, Your Majesty,' his advisers muttered. 'At least that is what we have heard.'

'But they were supposed to return to me! They were supposed to tell me where I could find this newborn king!'

'W-well, we know he's in Bethlehem,' said the advisers.

'Of course he's in Bethlehem!' the king shouted again. 'Along with hundreds of other babies…' And as soon as he'd said it, the king's face changed.

He no longer frowned.

He no longer scowled.

He no longer clenched his teeth or scrunched up his face.

No, King Herod began to smile – a dark and cruel smile.

'Leave me!' he commanded. 'And send in the captain of my guard.'

That smile was still on Herod's face when

the captain entered and bowed.

'I have a job for you,' the king explained.

'I want you to go to Bethlehem and kill…
oh, let us say, every male child two years old
and under.'

The captain did not smile.

He did not frown, either.

He just stood there with his lips pressed
tightly together.

His eyes showed his surprise, however, for this was the most awful thing he had ever heard.

'Well, get on with it!'the king commanded. 'You have your orders. And there are plenty of others,' he added, 'who would love to have your job.'

And so the captain left and rounded up his soldiers. And they set off to kill all of Bethlehem's baby boys.

Joseph slept. He had a sweet, sleepy smile on his face. But his smile turned to a worried frown when the visitor appeared to him in a dream. It was that busy angel, Gabriel, again. 'Get up, Joseph,' he said. 'Take the child and his mother and go to Egypt. Herod's soldiers are on the way. And they mean to kill the boy.'

Joseph got up at once. He nudged Mary awake and quietly they packed their things. Then she bundled up the sleeping Jesus and, together, they slipped off into the night.

They stayed in Egypt until King Herod died. Then they returned to Nazareth where Jesus grew up – the son of a carpenter and God's own special Son as well!

Printed in Great Britain
by Amazon

69470351R00040